For Jago

First published in Great Britain in 2005
by Zero To Ten Limited,
part of the Evans Publishing Group,
2A Portman Mansions, Chiltern Street, London W1U 6NR

British Library Cataloguing in Publication Data
Axworthy, Anni
The dragon who couldn't do dragony things
1. Dragons - Pictorial works - Juvenile fiction 2. Children's
stories - Pictorial works
I. Title
823.9'14 [J]

ISBN 1 840 89343 5

Printed in China

THE DRAGON WHO COULDN'T DO DRAGONY THINGS

written & illustrated by

ANNI AXWORTHY

A long time ago in a land of magic and mountains lived
Little Dragon.
He longed to be like the dragons of old that he read about
in storybooks: dragons that battled with knights on horseback,
dragons that flew from country to country, burning whole forests
with one breath of fire.

But although Little Dragon had wings, he didn't know how to fly. Although he had a snorty dragon nose he couldn't breathe fire, and because he was so small he didn't frighten anyone. He wasn't a very dragony dragon at all.

Little Dragon climbed to the top of a high mountain.
He was determined to learn to fly. He stood at the top
of the mountain, looked down, and started to run.
Slowly at first, then faster and faster –
he opened his wings, made a huge jump and . . .
landed with a hard bump.
And still he could not fly.

Little Dragon climbed onto the head of a very high statue and, with everyone watching, leaped. But his tail got in a tangle and the crowd of people watching below laughed and laughed as the little dragon swung gently from the sword.

Little Dragon decided to try to breathe fire. He put heaps of red-hot chilli peppers on his plate and covered that with more pepper.

Down it all went. His eyes started to bulge, his tummy rumbled, it shook – something was definitely happening! He opened his mouth really wide and let out an enormous **burp**. But no fire.

Little Dragon decided to be scary. He went to the woods and spent the whole day trying to frighten butterflies.

The butterflies just laughed and flew away.

Little Dragon stood in front of a puddle and practised making horrible faces. But when he tried to scare a baby, the baby gurgled and hit him with his teddy.

Little Dragon had tried and tried. Nothing had worked. He was cross and sad, and as he stomped home to his cave he started to cry – big hot angry tears. He got into bed, curled up in a tight little ball and cried himself to sleep.

Very early the next morning Little Dragon heard someone knocking at the door of his cave. In the dark he climbed down from what felt like a very hard and bumpy bed and went to see who had woken him up.

A boy was standing there, smiling. He had a basket over one arm.

"Hello. My name is Jago. I was in the woods looking for mushrooms when I found a trail of golden blobs. I've followed them all the way to your door."

Little Dragon looked at the ground. The path of golden blobs led to the door, through his legs and all the way to his bed.

Little Dragon stared and stared. What were these lumps of gold?
He picked them up – they were tear-shaped. Then he realised! He
had been weeping tears of gold. His bed had been hard because it
was filled with gold.

"What an incredible dragon you are," said Jago.

Little Dragon hung his head and looked very unhappy.
"No, I'm a useless dragon. I can't fly, I can't breathe
even a tiny spark of fire and nobody is ever afraid of me!"
Jago lifted the little dragon onto his lap
and gave him a cuddle.

"Who cares about that –
not every dragon cries like you!
Come and live with me.
My sister can be really scary.
She can show you how."

Little Dragon could think of nothing better. They gathered the golden tears in the basket and, carrying the heavy load together, they set off for Jago's home.

Jago's Mum was happy to have the dragon to stay. He didn't set fire to the curtains, flap in her way or frighten the postman. She didn't even mind that there were no mushrooms for tea.

Little Dragon never did learn to fly,

breathe fire or frighten babies, but now he never minded.

Every day all Jago's friends came to play with him.

He was so happy that he never cried another golden tear.

Jago's Mum put the golden tears safely away in the bank
and that summer Little Dragon flew for the very first time!